The Legend of Sun & Moon

THE ORIGIN STORY

KATIE MONOHAN

*In honor of the sacred stories we inherit—
the ones whispered before flame, and the
love that gave the universe its breath.*

The cultural significance of origins

Stories have always lived in my bones. As a Native American woman, I was raised with a deep reverence for the power of origins. Our creation stories aren't just tales. They're truths that shape identity, community, and belonging. They are how we remember who we are.

To begin a story without first honoring its roots would be to forget where it came from—and who it's for. So when I began crafting this series, *Celestial Bonds of Love*, I knew I couldn't move forward without first looking back. Before I could tell you the story of *Sun's Heart*—of Azalea, Atreyus, and the tangled bonds of love, fate, and sacrifice—I had to ask the questions that all true epics begin with:

Where did they come from?

How did they get here?

And what did they have to sacrifice in order to protect us?

I couldn't write a single meaningful word until I had those answers. Until I could feel the heartbeat of the cosmos echoing through my characters.

That's how *The Legend of the Sun and Moon* was born—a mythic tale rooted in love, sorrow, and celestial devotion. It became the soul of the world I was building. This legend isn't just background. It's the foundation. The memory. The marrow.

This isn't just fantasy—it's reclamation. A reminder that our stories are worthy of starlight, and our origins are worth retelling in every form they take.

Thank you for walking this path with me.

May you find light in the dark—and remember the sky you came from.

With love and moonlight,

Katie Monohan

The Legend of Sun & Moon

THE ORIGIN STORY

Primordial Times

Before day and night, before wind and fire, before the creation of the universe itself, life belonged solely to the Divine. They existed in a vast abyss, absent even the dimmest of lights.

That was until an idea fluttered into their thoughts in pursuit of some small purpose that could add meaning to their otherwise meaningless existences. It was only a tendril, softly tickling the edges of their minds. It was a concept that demanded delicate tending, for if it formed too quickly, it would be claimed by the void.

The Divine slowly danced around the idea, gently forming it until it started to take shape. When they were assured that it would not be sucked into the vast oblivion, they refined and sculpted it until it was a pristine work of art, at which point it seized their hearts and awakened their souls.

The idea was to fill the abyss with life.

The Divine were omnipotent beings, wielding the power to manifest anything within their imagination. There was indeed no end to their capabilities.

With unwavering determination, they embarked on creating the first celestial being. However, devoid of a spirit to bring it to life, the creation was sucked into obscurity, leaving behind only a black hole in its place.

Undeterred, they persisted in their endeavors, yet each attempt ended in failure and disappointment as the creation of life continuously eluded them.

In consolation of one another, the faintest touch ignited an unfamiliar warmth within them. A gentle exchange of breaths stirred a tremor of anticipation in their hearts. Their initial embraces were tentative, yet with each touch, their affection grew more confident until the flicker of admiration erupted into a passionate inferno of love.

Their adoration became the axis of their existence, an indispensable part of their being; to be without it would render them as hollow as the void itself.

From their ardor, a bond crystallized, cementing their devotion in their hearts and weaving their commitment to their souls.

In their native tongue, they called the bond "Vinfinitum," denoting infinite unity.

When they least expected, their fervor bore fruit, birthing the first generation of celestial beings: stars, planets, comets, satellites, and nebulae, thus transforming the abyss into an enchanting cosmos of endless beauty.

In its infancy, the universe was modest in scale, yet it was a radiant contrast to the emptiness of the void, captivating the Divine with the life they had bestowed upon it.

As time elapsed, love permeated the expanse of the aether. Satellites fell in love with planets, nebulae were captivated by stars, comets became infatuated with planets, and so forth, forging an intricate tapestry of affection.

The Divine nurtured the hope that their creation would flourish as love bloomed. However, a millennium passed, and despite the burgeoning affection, none of their progeny had sired offspring of their own. The Divine ached for their scions to procreate, ensuring their creation would live on. Otherwise, they feared the return of the desolation that once gripped the abyss.

After deep reflection, the Divine realized that the conception of their beloved celestials necessitated the creation of the Vinfinitum Bond—a bond of faith that transcended mere affection.

Love was the crucial foundation, but it also demanded strength to bolster each other's hopes and dreams and to provide support during moments of weakness.

It required wisdom to understand that perfection was an unattainable illusion, enabling them to embrace not only their partner's flaws but also their own.

It mandated courage to be vulnerable, fostering an environment where the tenderness of genuine intimacy could thrive.

Furthermore, it required faith in the other's reciprocal love and devotion. They had to believe that they would be cherished for all eternity, for the creation of life would bring unending responsibility.

Only when all five sacred virtues existed in harmony could the Vinfinitum Bond be formed.

The Divine recognized that their progeny each embodied one of the sacred virtues so entirely that it posed a challenge for them to embrace the others.

Stars radiated love, brightening the lives and hearts around them.

Planets stood resolute, emanating unwavering strength from their cores and serving as beacons of stability.

Comets brilliantly displayed wisdom, igniting insight and inspiration in the darkness as ideas flooded their minds.

Satellites were steadfast guardians, their unwavering courage deeply rooted in their souls as they orbited ever watchful and vigilant through the aether.

Nebulae stretched across the cosmos, breathtaking vistas of faith, inspiring boundless awe and wonder.

Realizing their heirs needed to embody all five sacred virtues in order to forge the Vinfinitum Bond, thus ensuring their ability to propagate their lineage, the Divine felt compelled to devise a strategy to rectify their deficiencies.

Believing that mutual sharing of the associated blessings was the most effective method to inspire the requisite qualities, the Divine approached their cherished celestials with a proposition. In exchange for their solemn vow to disseminate the wonders of their virtues across the universe, the Divine were prepared to bestow upon them otherworldly powers to assist in their mission.

As their progeny eagerly embraced the opportunity to enrich the lives of others, the Divine faithfully fulfilled their promise.

Stars were graced with the gift of empathy, which enabled them to cultivate love when combined with the inherent adoration within their hearts.

Planets were endowed with strength transference, granting them the ability to lend strength to others.

Comets were bestowed retrocognition, empowering them to delve into intricate subjects such as mathematics, science, history, language, and the arts, and share their wisdom across the universe.

Satellites received the gift of power ascendancy, allowing them to instill courage in others. However, it was a formidable ability that they were entrusted to wield prudently due to its profound potential for peril.

Nebulae, having been tasked with imbuing faith, a virtue arduous to inspire, for it required believing in something without the assurance of evidence, were bequeathed with space/time manipulation, allowing them to traverse the cosmos to foster faith without the hindrance of time.

With their mystical gifts, the celestials influenced one another, resulting in the evolution of varying degrees of other virtues. In time, they may have amply evolved to create the Vinfinitum Bond.

However, the celestials were not known for their patience and sought alternative solutions for their inability to procreate.

They stumbled upon a revelation: if representatives of each of the five virtues bestowed their blessing during a commitment ritual, they could forge the Vinfinitum Bond as if they wholly possessed all five virtues themselves.

The tradition of commitment rituals quickly spread throughout the universe, giving rise to ensuing generations of celestial beings.

As the Divine's descendants multiplied, life in the cosmos began to resemble the contemporary society that would eventually be known to humans on Earth. Celestials coexisted harmoniously, forging friendships, falling in love, and starting families. They were sentient beings, driven by emotions, experiencing happiness and sorrow, possessing fears and desires.

Although some desires were noble enough to nurture life, others were so malevolent they wrought death.

part one

Eternal Love

Sun and Moon belonged to a clan in Andromeda comprised of five interconnected families with ties spanning generations. Despite their dissimilar personalities, they had been close for the entirety of their lives. Their connection transcended mere companionship. An unspoken understanding between them hinted at something more profound than friendship.

Sun was intelligent, beautiful, and the most caring being in the universe. Her love for others was more fervent than anyone had ever known. She was the true incarnation of love and, thus, loved by many.

Conversely, Moon was strong, honorable, and brave but not necessarily tenderhearted. He had an air of confidence that was rightly earned through discipline and hard work, and though he was admired and respected, he was only genuinely loved by few.

Still, Sun and Moon were inseparable, dedicating every available moment to each other.

In their youth, Sun and Moon engaged in innocent mischief, delighting in playful tricks on each other and their unsuspecting friends and family. As they matured, they became pillars of support, nurturing one another through the journey of self-discovery and inspiring each other in their individual pursuits for experience and knowledge.

Moon's feelings for Sun shifted imperceptibly over time, their transformation so gradual that he couldn't pinpoint the moment he fell in love.

With each passing day, his adoration for her intensified until it became a deep, eternal love. When Moon finally realized the profound depth of his emotions, he was enamored.

Clinging to hope, he longed for Sun to reciprocate his affection and accept him as her suitor. However, propriety dictated that Moon would be forbidden to commence courting until his older brother, Draugr, chose a mate. This tradition was intended to preserve familial harmony and prevent discord within households.

Consumed by thoughts of Sun and unable to focus on anything other than his beloved, Moon sought solace and guidance from his close friends, Arrod and Keid, who he found with Sedna, one of his three cherished sisters.

As fate would have it, upon confessing his feelings for Sun, Arrod revealed that he, too, harbored feelings for her. Sun, who had always been a close confidant of both Moon and Arrod, was caught in the middle of their unexpected discovery.

This revelation left Moon stunned, as he had been sure of Arrod's feelings for Sun's dear friend. "What about Giada?" Moon inquired, struggling to accept the unforeseen development.

"What about her?" Arrod's confusion was apparent, leading

Moon to believe he had been utterly mistaken in Arrod's regard for Giada.

"I was under the impression that you had feelings for her," Moon admitted, unable to fathom the idea of sharing romantic feelings for the same woman as his friend. Desperate to dispel any misconceptions, he continued, "You and Giada seem so perfectly matched, so alike in many ways."

"How do you figure?" Arrod inquired, puzzled by Moon's assertion. "I fail to see any similarities between Giada and me. She is a satellite, whereas I am a nebula. If anything, you and Giada share more similarities than she and I do."

"Hardly! You are both outgoing and charismatic," Moon observed. "Whereas I tend to be more reserved, austere, and ordinary. Keid, Sedna, would you not agree?" he probed, seeking validation from their mutual friends.

"You're anything but ordinary," Keid teased, hinting at Moon's unique qualities while subtly acknowledging the other attributes.

"Keid!" Sedna admonished, shooting a disapproving glance at her soon-to-be mate before addressing Arrod. "You do share similar personality traits with Giada," she agreed with her brother, understanding his desire to redirect Arrod's affection, though she knew it was futile.

"I suppose we are much the same in personality. Too much the same, perhaps. I care for Giada as a cherished friend, but it is Sun who has captured my heart."

Moon found himself at a crossroads, uncertain of the path ahead. He understood that Sun couldn't possibly reciprocate their feelings in a way they each desired, nor would they wish for such a predicament.

Moreover, there was no assurance that Sun harbored affection for either of them, he admitted to himself. Yet, amidst this swirling uncertainty, one conviction remained steadfast in his mind.

"Regardless of the outcome, we must safeguard our rapport above all," Moon urged, emphasizing the paramount importance he placed on their friendship.

"If Sun were to choose one of us, wouldn't that inevitably strain our camaraderie?" Arrod questioned, voicing his concern.

Being as she was a comet, Sedna was inherently wise and offered her guidance.

"What purpose does it serve for the unlucky of you to object?" she questioned. "That would only condemn Sun to a life of unhappiness. If you truly love her, as you both profess, you would not want her to be discontented."

Sedna paused, allowing her words to sink in as she observed her brother and friend. Sensing their agreement with her reasoning, she continued, "However, if you both bless the union with whoever secures her affection, the other will undoubtedly contribute to ensuring her eternal happiness."

"I won't pretend it will be effortless, but is it not preferable to the alternative?" Moon posed in earnest. "If Sun decides to bestow her heart upon one of us, can we doubt that the chosen would show compassion toward his ill-fated friend?"

"And you are capable of this? Are you sure you're not just feeling overly confident, my friend?" Arrod inquired skeptically. "It's simple to consider if you think of yourself as the victor, but can you truly imagine this commitment from the perspective of the one less favored?"

"Yes, I am not as confident as you believe. If Sun should choose you, I will give you my blessing," Moon affirmed sincerely.

"And you would stand by and watch as we forge the Vinfinitum Bond?"

"Yes, I would strive to accept my fate and hold onto the hope of finding happiness someday, as I wouldn't want to lose either of you. It would undoubtedly be arduous, but I have the courage to confront it," Moon declared with unwavering determination.

"And I will be by your side to offer strength and support," Keid added reassuringly for the benefit of both his friends.

"I admit I may not possess the same level of courage as you, but I have faith," Arrod expressed to Moon, reaching out to embrace his friend warmly.

That simple exchange sealed their vow of friendship. Should Sun reciprocate the feelings of either, the one disfavored would gracefully accept their fate, prioritizing Sun's happiness above their own. However, unbeknownst to Moon and Arrod, other contenders were vying for Sun's affection.

part TWO

Inner Strength

Eager to secure Sun's love, Moon approached his brother, Draugr, who had recently returned from some travels. He sought to persuade Draugr to take a mate, thus allowing him to court Sun. Moon poured his heart out to his brother, expressing his deep love and desire for the one he cherished to accept him.

Moon disclosed the rivalry between himself and his friend, explaining they shared a longing for the affection of the same woman.

Arrod had only one sibling, Elias, who happened to be his twin, so no barriers would prevent him from pursuing the one they both adored.

Moon confessed his fear to Draugr, expressing that if he were not allowed to commence courting, Arrod posed an imminent threat of winning his beloved's affection and implored him to understand the urgency of his situation.

"What a lucky coincidence that you should mention it, for there is something I wish to discuss with you," Draugr remarked, pausing in his tasks to give his full attention to his younger brother. "I will be taking a mate very soon."

"Really?" Moon's excitement soared, anticipating he would finally be allowed to start courting Sun.

However, his hopes were crushed upon hearing his brother's next words.

"Yes, I have taken a fancy to Sun. Father has initiated negotiations with her family, and we are nearing an agreement. I anticipate she will be mine very soon, which brings me to what I wanted to discuss with you. I know you two have grown quite close while I was away, thus I wish for you to recommend me to her."

"Sun? My Sun?" Moon exclaimed, horror and disbelief gripping his words.

"Yes, your friend, Sun," he said, with a pointed emphasis on the word "friend."

Moon's worst nightmare was unfolding before him, yet he refused to succumb to despair. Instead, he delved deep into the recesses of his being, searching for his inner strength. "No! I will not recommend you to her! You cannot possibly love her! You have been gone for many years. She was but a child when you departed on your journey."

"Ah, but she has blossomed into the most exquisite being in the entire universe, for I should know, having traversed much of it," Draugr countered, convincing Moon that his desire for Sun stemmed from purely physical motives, driven by her outward beauty rather than any genuine emotional connection.

"Indeed, but you scarcely know her. You are unfamiliar with her joys and sorrows. You're ignorant of her fears and desires."

"For your sake, young Moon, I pray the object of your affection is not my Sun." With a forceful tone, he once again emphasized the keyword in his speech, "my," then continued, "for I fear you will be broken-hearted. Commitment rules are clear and favor the eldest son."

"But you have not courted her. Surely, she would not agree to accept you."

"Courting is not necessary for a commitment to be arranged. Sun's family has the authority to secure a union for her. However, let me be clear. I have every intention of courting her."

"If that is the case, why would you not first secure her affection naturally. Are you afraid she might reject you?"

"I have my reasons, and I need not explain them to you. The fact remains that it is my right to choose first."

"Draugr, I implore you. You must understand the depth of my feelings for Sun. She is my closest confidante. She is the one I love." Moon pleaded with his elder brother, but Draugr remained unsympathetic, consumed by his own desires.

"And you are certain she returns your affection?" Draugr inquired.

"Yes!" Moon exclaimed, but his faith soon faltered. "Well, perhaps more hopeful than certain."

"I will make you a deal. Because you are my brother, I will give you one chance to prove she returns your affection. I will relinquish my claim on Sun if you can persuade her to kiss you before Arrod and me at the celebration of Sedna's commitment with Keid tomorrow evening."

"Arrod?" Moon questioned. "What involvement does he have in this?"

"He is also in love with her, is he not?"

"Yes, but—"

"Sun's Divine Gift of empathy makes her naturally compassionate," Draugr interjected, anticipating Moon's question. "If she senses Arrod's affection for her, she may refrain from kissing you in front of him to avoid causing him pain. However, if she is deeply in love with you, she will be so captivated by your presence in the romantic setting that she won't even notice Arrod's feelings. Consequently, she will not hesitate to share a kiss with you."

"Fine... I agree." Moon wasn't sure if he could coax a kiss from Sun in just one evening, especially with Arrod also vying for her affection, but what other option did he have? It was his only hope. Thus, driven by his unwavering love for Sun, Moon acceded to Draugr's treaty, for the thought of losing her was utterly unbearable.

"You have not heard the conditions of the treaty," Draugr insisted.

"It matters not," Moon replied dismissively, knowing that arguing with Draugr would only make his demands more stringent. "Anything to please you," he added, his heart heavy with the weight of his love for Sun.

"The conditions are these," Draugr asserted firmly. "You must not speak of your love for her, either before or during the celebration. You must not disclose our treaty to anyone. And if she fails to kiss you before Sedna and Keid depart for the evening, you will leave Andromeda forever and never return."

"Leave Andromeda?"

"Yes, leave Andromeda! I cannot have you lingering around, pining for my mate, now, can I?" Draugr affirmed.

Moon pondered the treaty's terms, his heart heavy with conflicting emotions. The prospect of banishment from his home and everyone he loved was unthinkable, yet it was a fate better than a life without his beloved Sun.

"Are we in agreement?" His brother pressed with urgency and impatience, breaking through Moon's inner struggle.

Recognizing there was no room for negotiations, Moon answered with a sense of resignation, his voice barely above a whisper, "Yes, if it is my only opportunity, I will seize it. It is certainly preferable to having no chance at all."

"In return, I will make you a promise," Draugr declared with a patronizing tone, his narrowed eyes betraying his growing irritation. "If she does kiss you, I will leave Andromeda and never return." He stood tall with his chest puffed out after invading Moon's space to assert dominance over his brother.

"Then we are to be brothers no more?" Moon's brow furrowed with confusion and sadness.

"You could give up this foolish notion and accept what is." Draugr retorted, contempt lining his cadence.

Recalling his sister's logic, he remarked, "Do you not wish for Sun's happiness? Denying her the love she feels for me will be condemning her to a life devoid of affection if such love exists. Surely, such an outcome is not what you desire for her."

"What alternative is there?" Draugr shrugged indifferently, dismissing his brother's concern.

Still immersed in the memory of his conversation with his friends, Moon thought about the vow with Arrod, but something told him that Draugr would not be interested in the same. It could have been Draugr's aggressive tone or the challenge in his eyes that begged for acceptance. Regardless, Moon knew Draugr was motivated not to secure Sun's happiness but rather to fulfill his own desires.

part three

Broken Faith

Impatient to see his beloved, Moon arrived early at the celebration the following evening, his anticipation palpable despite his subdued demeanor. Shortly thereafter, Draugr emerged with Giada by his side, a smug look adorning his countenance as if he harbored knowledge unknown to Moon. There was no doubt that Draugr invited Giada to accompany him as she was one of Sun's dearest friends, and since she had no siblings, she would be pleased to receive the offer of an escort.

While Moon waited for Sun, Keid arrived accompanied by Arrod, Elias, and Moon's youngest sister, Syia. Moon warmly greeted Keid as the guest of honor with a respectful bow. He couldn't help but notice Elias holding Syia a little too closely, but with other pressing matters on his mind, Moon chose not to address the issue.

When Arrod greeted Moon, the urge to inform him of the treaty with Draugr tugged at his thoughts. However, he refrained, mindful of the conditions that forbade disclosure. Arrod inquired as to the reason Moon had yet to join the celebration, and Moon explained that he was awaiting Sun's arrival. Unwilling to allow Moon such an advantage, Arrod decided to wait with him, much to Moon's disappointment.

Sun's brother, Lynd, finally arrived, accompanied by another of Moon's sisters, Sedna's twin, Dhava. Moon hurriedly greeted them as he was eager to welcome Sun, whom he had imagined arriving with Lynd. Moon's gaze swept the area in anticipation of Sun's presence. However, Lynd informed him that Sun would not be attending the celebration as she was consoling their sister, who was suffering from a broken heart. Having been rejected by a lover, Helia was not fit to be seen in society.

"I was unaware Helia had formed an attachment with someone," Moon stated in response to the news. Given the intimate bond shared between their households, he was convinced he would have been honored with such intelligence.

"No, nor I," Lynd admitted. "She has been quite exemplary in her discretion."

"Will you not acknowledge your sister?" Dhava inquired, having been disregarded long enough.

"Forgive me, My Dear Dhava. You look lovely this evening," Moon said after being prompted. He was not intentionally ignoring his sister. The news of Sun's absence had just filled him with trepidation. "Pray, I humbly request your pardon and seek your kind release."

Upon receiving Dhava's approving nod, Moon expeditiously sought out Draugr to relay the news of Sun's supposed absence. He pleaded with his brother to extend the time to satisfy the terms of their treaty, but Draugr was unmoved by his angst and denied his request.

Moon left the celebration and hastened to find Sun, only to encounter Helia instead. In Moon's estimation, she did appear to be distraught, so he kept the conversation brief and asked if she would deliver a letter to Sun. Moon longed to profess his love for her in his missive, but mindful of the terms of the treaty, he carefully chose his words.

My Dear Sun,

As I eagerly awaited your arrival at the commitment celebration for Sedna and Keid, I received word from Lynd of your unavoidable absence. My heart longs to see you. I understand you are tending to your sister's heartache, but I implore you to meet me at the celebration. I cannot say what shall happen if I am denied the pleasure of your companionship tonight; the consequence is too much to bear.

With my everlasting heart,

Moon

Moon returned to the celebration, his demeanor marked by anxious anticipation. He abstained from dancing or engaging in conversation, focusing solely on what he hoped would be Sun's imminent arrival.

Merriments enlivened as Sedna and Keid announced their retirement for the evening, but Moon could not join in the delight. Debilitating despair sank into his heart as he watched his dreams fade away with Sedna and Keid.

Shortly after the couple's departure, Helia approached, fidgeting nervously as she presented Moon with a letter. "Sun asked me to deliver this to you," she explained.

Perplexed, Moon questioned, "If you are sick with heartache, why would Sun ask you to deliver a letter to me?"

"Just read it," Helia urged in a soothing voice, her expression softened with empathy.

Dear Moon,

I have never felt more sincere than I do now as I write these words: you are genuinely a cherished friend. I have suspected you have taken a romantic interest in me for some time. I see now that it has come to pass that I must inform you, most compassionately, that I am in love with Draugr, and our fathers are negotiating our commitment. Having learned of your treaty with my beloved, I purposefully stayed away from the celebration so as not to give you false hope. I made up the story of Helia's heartbreak as an excuse to save me from attending tonight. My beautiful sister was gracious enough to go along with my tale and selfless enough to deny herself the pleasure of attending the celebration. I do hope we can remain close friends.

With amity,

Sun

Moon's hopes and desires shattered like delicate crystals under intense pressure upon reading Sun's letter, leaving him breathless, his heart heavy with the weight of broken faith.

23

part four

Cunning Deceit

Upon Draugr's return to Andromeda, Helia entrusted him with the knowledge of her secret affection for Moon, thereby gaining his trust. In turn, Draugr confided in her his intention to sever the connection between his brother and her sister. Seeking her assistance, he assured her that Sun would not hinder her union with Moon if they collaborated in their efforts. Sufficiently piqued by Draugr's proposition, Helia had ardently agreed to assist in any way she could.

Several hours before Sedna and Keid's commitment ceremony, Draugr approached Helia with the details of the treaty he had brokered with Moon and his strategy to separate him from Sun. Fully embracing Draugr's plan, veiled in cunning deceit, Helia executed the initial phase with precision, preventing Sun from attending the romantic event.

As Sedna and Keid retired from the celebration, Helia seized the moment, deliberately positioning herself in Moon's path to deliver a letter seemingly from Sun. She was hoping Moon would seek to withdraw from Andromeda promptly after reading her carefully composed missive.

"Moon? Are you alright?" Helia asked, striving to convey genuine concern in response to his visible distress. Leaning in slightly, she offered a gentle touch as a silent gesture of support.

"I beg your pardon, Helia. Be assured, I shall be well," he murmured, forcing a semblance of calm into his voice. "Kindly convey my regards to Sun. Let her know that I hope she will be quite content with Draugr."

"I will deliver your message, but why not convey these sentiments yourself when next you see her?" Helia feigned innocence, crafting a mask to hide any hint of her true intentions.

"I... I cannot," Moon faltered, his resolve succumbing to the pain of unspoken truths. "I must go."

"What? Why? Go where?" Helia portrayed an air of oblivion to Moon's impending departure with subtle yet deliberate gestures.

"I know not, but I am afraid I must leave Andromeda."

"Leave Andromeda?" Once again, the façade was executed perfectly. "Allow me to accompany you! I long to leave Andromeda and discover the rest of the universe," Helia pleaded in earnest, determination clear in her tone.

"I fear I will not make a joyful companion," Moon confessed, his gaze filled with grief.

"Let me be the light amidst your darkness," Helia implored, reaching out to embrace him in solidarity.

Moon eventually relented, despite his reluctance, but was adamant about departing directly, leaving no time for Helia to bid farewell to her family. Consequently, she settled on sending a letter to her sister.

My Dearest Sister,

I must express my deepest gratitude for your unwavering presence, which offered solace as I tended to the wounds of my broken heart. After much contemplation, I resolved to attend the ceremony of Sedna and Keid's commitment, trusting in its vivacity to uplift my spirits. It was a merry occasion, one I am sure you would have wished not to miss. I deeply regret my decision to depart without forewarning, thus depriving you of the joyous merriment. Evening had already set in when I resolved to join the festivities, and I was loath to trouble you with the task of readying yourself after persuading you to remain at my side.

Yet, amidst my regret, I have blissful tidings to share. At the celebration, I chanced upon Moon, and the news he shared with me shall surely astonish you. He embarks on a quest for thrilling adventures, disillusioned by the mundane confines of our home in Andromeda. His departure is imminent, and to my delight, he has extended to me an invitation to accompany him. We shall depart forthwith upon the completion of this missive.

Oh, Dear Sister, my heart overflows with jubilation! I cannot fathom remaining in Andromeda after the heartbreak I have endured. Moon assures me that the man he deemed a fool is unworthy of my affection. Please convey my fond

Despite the deceit woven into Helia's words, they achieved the objective of reassuring her family about her safe departure, with the added benefit of planting seeds of doubt regarding Moon's affection for Sun.

Driven by her determination not to miss the opportunity to journey with Moon as his exclusive companion, she swiftly dispatched the letter, notwithstanding its inconsistencies.

Upon settling in their initial destination, Helia promptly wrote to Sun, providing the promised instructions for correspondence. Soon after sending the information, she received a letter in return.

*myself struggling to comprehend his sudden departure
with you, especially considering my expectation that
he was soon to make an offer of commitment to me. I
cannot help but wonder if his heart remains true to me
or if he has taken a sudden interest in you, and I find
myself in need of confirmation regarding his intentions.*

*Rest assured, Dearest Helia, I have
unwavering faith in our sisterly affection and do not
believe you would betray me in such a manner. I am
confident that your departure with Moon is solely
motivated by your desire to escape the heartache that has
befallen you, and I wish you nothing but the best in your
explorations. Your happiness and well-being are of the
utmost importance to me. However, I do hope for your
swift return following the mending of your heart.*

*As you venture into this new chapter of your life,
please know that my thoughts and well wishes will always
accompany you. May your adventures be filled with joy,
excitement, and endless possibilities. Though physical
distance may separate us, our sisterhood remains
unbreakable.*

With all my love and heartfelt wishes,

Sun

Accompanying Helia's epistle was a second letter intended for Moon. However, with a measure of audacity, Helia took it upon herself to peruse its contents.

My Dearest Moon,

I trust this correspondence finds you in good spirits, though a certain unease weighs heavily upon my heart. The sudden departure of both yourself and my dear sister has left me in a state of profound perplexity and apprehension.

You must know you hold an irreplaceable position in my heart, and the prospect of your absence casts a shadow upon my soul that cannot easily be dispelled.

I find myself entangled in a web of unanswered questions regarding the circumstances surrounding your sudden vanishing. Might I venture to inquire as to the cause of your unexpected parting? I possess an ardent desire for elucidation. I yearn to comprehend the truth behind your decision and its implications for what I believe to be our burgeoning relationship.

Your steadfast presence and unwavering support have been a source of immeasurable comfort and joy. While I am not unsympathetic to your thirst for adventure, I had allowed myself to entertain the hope, nay, the conviction that our attachment was evolving into something far more profound and intimate. Thus, upon learning of your expedition in the company of my sister, I could not suppress a pang of disquietude, having deemed our connection to be of a more tender nature than mere friendship. I held our shared moments and expressions of affection as signs of a deeper bond between us.

Your departure without a word of farewell has left me questioning the veracity of my sentiments. Assuredly, My Dearest, your absence will be keenly felt. I can only pray that this separation proves to be of short duration.

I eagerly await your reply in the fervent hope that it may provide some measure of understanding and resolution to assuage the tumult within my breast. Until your return, I remain with a heavy heart and bated breath.

Though I am loath to commit these sentiments to paper, I find myself compelled to express the depth of my feelings in your absence. I love you, My Dearest Moon. I shall love you for all eternity.

With my eternal love,

Sun

"Insufferable," Helia exclaimed, her voice quivering indignantly as she cast the offending letter into the flames. She refused to tolerate Sun's impudent endeavors to seize what she rightfully deemed her own. Verily, in her view, a partner ought to be esteemed as the rightful possession of a lover. Having yet to secure Moon's love was inconsequential. Fixed on addressing the matter with Draugr and resolved to have him fulfill his end of the accord in separating her sister from his brother, she clenched her pen with fierce determination.

Dear Draugr,

I should think that you'd like to commend me for the successful execution of our scheme thus far. By orchestrating Sun's absence from the festivities under the guise of my affliction, I have not only facilitated Moon's departure from Andromeda but also dispelled Sun's belief in Moon's affection for her.

Pray, enlighten me on the current state of affairs in your realm. How do you fare in your relations with my sister? You may be astonished to learn that on the day I received a missive from Sun, Moon also received correspondence from her. Fortunately, I intercepted the epistle. I had hoped Sun would have redirected her affections toward you by now, as such a development would have alleviated my concerns regarding her potential interference in my endeavors to capture Moon's heart. I trust you comprehend the diverse benefits such a progression would offer, transcending mere personal interests.

Please write and advise me on the most prudent course of action.

Yours sincerely,

Helia

Helia anxiously awaited Draugr's reply, fearful of acting without his counsel, but to her relief, it finally came.

Dear Helia,

Your concern, though noted, seems exaggerated. I trust you can manage the task of attending to the post and disposing of any correspondence meant for my brother. Should this prove burdensome, consider informing your family of your acquaintance with a gentleman and your decision to part ways with Moon. Such action would effectively cut off all communication with him.

Regarding my relationship with Sun, rest assured that an invitation to my forthcoming commitment ceremony will be extended in due time. Until then, refrain from further correspondence with me. However, promptly return the missive from Sun. She has expressed her concern about not hearing from you. I did not think I should have to tell you that it is imperative for you to maintain amicable correspondence with her. This is crucial for all parties involved.

-Draugr

Following Draugr's advice, Helia continued to correspond with Sun. When checking the post became too troublesome, she wrote to her family, informing them she had moved on from Moon as her respected travel companion, having met someone and fallen in love.

part five

Enlightening Wisdom

Time elapsed slowly, each moment deepening Moon's misery. The special moments he spent with Sun turned into distant memories, and Moon found himself battered by the trials of time. He was distraught over the loss of Sun. The mere thought of her with his brother relentlessly tormented him. He pondered her fate nonstop, wondering if she was happy, if she and his brother had borne children, if she ever reminisced about their time as close companions.

As signs of age began distinguishing themselves upon his features, Moon wrote Sun a letter, despite his efforts to leave her in peace. He did not anticipate correspondence in return, yet a glimmer of hope dared to flicker in his heart.

My Dear Sun,

I have begun the composition of this correspondence countless times since last I had the pleasure of your camaraderie. While convention would dictate inquiries into your commitment with Draugr and divulgence of hope that it has gratified you chiefly, candor prohibits such disingenuous conveyance.

In my quest for solace from the void left by your absence, I've roamed the universe in pursuit of adventures. Despite the myriad experiences, none have assuaged the ache of losing you.

Helia has been an unexpectedly pleasant companion amidst my travels. I often hope she will bring news of you, but I am disheartened by her lack of information, as is always the case. I think she keeps me ignorant of your circumstances so as not to cause me pain. However, any amount of agony would be inconsequential to the torture of living without you. It could certainly not overshadow the felicity of learning of you. Even still, being as Helia is your sister, having her near offers a semblance of closeness to you.

Sleep eludes me, and when it finally comes, I dream only of you. I dream of the long days I worked for your father just to be near you. I dream of the times you visited my sisters and how I would steal glimpses of you. I dream of when you taught me to dance and how I pretended to be inept to prolong the time with you in my embrace.

What I would not give to look upon your beauty, hear the melody of your song, breathe in the fragrance of your soft scent, and, most of all, feel the warmth of your touch. I took these gifts for granted, but the desolating calamity of my existence lies in never having the pleasure of knowing the sweetness of your kiss.

Without you, the universe holds no allure. I know not how to go on. I write not to vex you, and I wish not to cause you pain, but I can ignore the cries of my heart no longer, for the cries have turned into wails, the wails have turned into shrieks, and the shrieks will not be unheeded.

I am quite certain that I shall never again know the joy and comfort of your companionship, but is it iniquitous to hope for correspondence? Nothing in my oath imposes such restriction, though I know not what shall govern your decision on the matter. You should know that I would be eager to receive your letters if it should please you to write. I am currently situated and receiving posts in Milky Way, as you may already know from your correspondence with Helia.

I find that I cannot conclude this letter without laying bare my feelings for you with unequivocal clarity. My Dear Sun, I love you. I have been, and always will be, in love with you.

With my everlasting heart,

Moon

Moon had contemplated how to conclude his letter but resolved, somewhat hastily, to bare his soul and regretted it almost immediately. For what foolishness had possessed him? Sun had openly declared her affection for his brother and even forged the Vinfinitum Bond with him.

With his correspondence irretrievably sent, Moon was in dire need of strength to endure, a virtue that felt even more arduous to invoke.

Before long, Moon found himself in possession of a reply.

As he beheld the seal adorning the epistle, his heart hastened with anticipation, torn between optimism and trepidation. Though he dared to entertain the futile hope of a warm reception to his letter, he feared encountering a missive akin to the one he had received on the eve of Sedna and Keid's commitment celebration.

After ensuring his solitude, he broke the seal and inspected the contents.

Dearest Moon,

Long have I awaited tidings from you, and I had almost despaired. Your letter brings both solace and dismay, revealing a grievous misconception. I am not bonded to your brother, nor to any other. Though Draugr calls upon me often, beseeching me to accept him, my answer remains the same. I cannot form the Vinfinitum Bond with him, for my heart belongs to you.

As it has been many years since you called Andromeda your home, Draugr now suggests that I

consider him as an alternative to my solitude. He deems
it certain that you will remain lost to us, convinced you
have embarked on a life of exploration. He opines that
perhaps one day you shall return, but only after finding
the one who tames your wild heart and captures your
adventurous soul.

I have maintained correspondence with Helia,
but I was unaware of your continued travels with my
sister. She had conveyed that she left Andromeda with
you originally but remained by your side only briefly.
Some time ago, she wrote informing her family that
she met someone with whom she fell madly in love and
intended to travel the universe alongside her chosen
suitor, though she had omitted her lover's name. I
now understand the reason for her prevarication in the
matter.

Moreover, I know not of any oath you have
given that should prevent correspondence between us. I
wrote to you frequently, ceasing only when I presumed
my sister was no longer accompanying you. Although,
I suspect you have never received any of my letters.

As I reflect on these obscurities, I am filled
with trepidation as it appears that inauspicious forces
conspire to keep us apart.

I had hoped your heart discerned the depth of my
affection for you. However, as you are able to fathom
me bonded to another, I know now it did not.

Upon reading the letter, Moon's heart quickened its pace. He longed to behold Sun again but knew not how, as he had sworn never to return to Andromeda. His sole recourse lay in her calling upon him in Milky Way. However, could he beseech her to forsake her family and friends for him? Could he dare make such entreaties? If the circumstances were reversed, he would unhesitatingly comply. But could she harbor the same fervent love for him that he held for her? Could she ache for his presence as ardently as he pined for hers?

Despite the rush of adrenaline, fueled by the enlightening wisdom gleaned from Sun's letter, Moon was resolved to promptly compose a response and plead with her to join him in Milky Way. However, as soon as he put his pen to the parchment, he was interrupted.

"Leave!" he snapped at the messenger. "You disrupt my solitude."

"Might you spare a twinkling for an old friend?" Sun answered somewhat tentatively.

Moon's countenance underwent a swift transformation, and

he turned abruptly to behold the face that matched the voice. "Sun! My Dearest Sun! Can it be you?"

"Yes, Moon. It is I who have journeyed here to see you." She took a hesitant step toward him, testing his reaction.

Moon pulled Sun close in a tight embrace, his gaze filled with desire. "But... how? I received your letter only just. You could not possibly have traveled with such haste."

Sun cupped Moon's face, returning his glance with longing. "I harbored fears that my letter might be intercepted, so I have come to ensure that my sentiments were received."

"But the journey from Andromeda would take—"

Arrod escorted me," she said, excitement overwhelming her as she interrupted him. Her words implied that Arrod had used his Divine-given power over space to transport her to Milky Way, free from the constraints of time. "I would have come sooner, but it took time to persuade our friend to oblige my request, for he feared my honored character would be tainted by the act."

"I was in the midst of composing a response to your letter, entreating you to join me here in Milky Way." He returned her tender gesture by caressing her soft cheek. "You must permit me to express that I have never felt such joy as I do in this moment."

Finally succumbing to the longing that had possessed him for as long as he could remember, Moon leaned in, capturing Sun's lips in a passionate, lingering kiss, his heart overflowing with affection and yearning. The kiss began fervently, almost desperate, but soft-ened into something tender, tranquil, and deeply affectionate.

Time seemed to slip away as Moon held Sun in an ardent embrace, the world fading away as he was consumed by the inten-sity of their connection. Their first kiss finally came to fruition after what felt like an eternity of pining for the warmth of her touch. Reluctantly, he broke away, a pang of longing tugging at his heart, as he remembered his manners and inquired about her well-being.

"Has your journey left you fatigued? May I offer you any comfort?" he asked, seeking to make amends for his earlier negligence arising from the initial shock of seeing her.

"No, I am not fatigued," she chuckled, her eyes alight with joy. "And I require nothing but your affection." She gently kissed his handsome face, a silent reassurance of their affection lingering in the air.

"Does your family know you have come to visit me?" he asked with reluctance, preferring their silence to be filled with kisses rather than conversation.

"No, I persuaded Arrod to accompany me here in secrecy. I don't think I would have succeeded in my endeavor if it were not for his eagerness to see you."

"Arrod! My good friend. How is he?"

"He misses you."

"Does he..." Moon stopped, fearing that speaking the words that plagued him would render them forsaken.

Sun observed his hesitation and finished his question, "Does he know that I am in love with you?"

Moon nodded and softly inquired, "Does he?"

"He does. I am not ignorant of his feelings for me. He sought to court me shortly after your departure, but I informed him of my affection for you, just as I had your brother. Arrod accepted that my heart belonged to you, though Draugr never assented. Arrod never broached the subject of his affection for me again—not earnestly, anyway, and he has remained my closest companion."

"How are Sedna and Keid?" he asked out of a sense of politeness.

"They are as enamored as ever, but surely you know this."

"No, I have sent correspondence, but I believe Sedna and Keid are vexed with me."

"Moon—"

Sun started, but Moon did not desire sympathy, so he continued asking after their friends. "And what of Giada?"

"It's quite incredulous, but Giada has developed feelings for Draugr. He is oblivious to her affection, causing her presence to go unnoticed. The dynamic of Giada's longing for Draugr's attention, combined with his fondness for me, has introduced a layer of complexity to our interactions, leading to an unfortunate decline in our conversations. Truthfully, it pains me to acknowledge that our friendship has suffered as a result."

"I'm sorry to hear such solemn news."

"I confess it does fill me with sorrow, but I have had little choice but to come to peace with the situation."

"Does she still engage with Arrod?"

"On occasion, but her focus is set on gaining Draugr's attention."

"So, Draugr still seeks your favor?"

"Perhaps we should make haste. Arrod must return soon," she interjected, though it did not seem to be a deliberate evasion of his inquiry.

"No, please. You arrived only just. My heart cannot endure the deprivation again so soon."

"You mistake me, my love. It is my intention to stay with you, if you will have me. However, Arrod must return. I should not wish his participation in my elopement to be known."

"Should you not return with Arrod?" he asked.

"If that is your desire," she acceded, though she knew it was not.

"I wish you never to leave, but it would be improper for you to stay when we are not bonded to each other. I will not be the cause of shame falling upon you."

"There is a solution that will allow me to stay that would not cause me shame."

Moon understood that she meant for them to forge the Vinfinitum Bond, which was Moon's only desire. "Without family? Without ceremony? I wish not to deprive you of these delights. Nor do I know anyone in Milky Way who could represent the virtues."

"I do not care about ceremony. I care only for you." She paused and looked as though she was concentrating on something. "Moon, we do not need anyone else to represent the virtues. We can create the Vinfinitum Bond ourselves."

"Without the blessings of all five virtues, it is impossible. However, if you go now, I will make haste and gather the representatives. Then, when you return, our union will be proper."

"I am an empath, attuned to the virtues residing within us. Our own essences will infuse our union with love and courage. Furthermore, you also possess enough strength, and I wisdom, allowing us to bestow these virtues upon our commitment as well."

"And what of faith?" Moon asked, not to dissuade his beloved, but practically, he could not foresee a solution.

"Arrod will bless our union with faith," she replied, and the answer was so obvious that Moon was not sure how he did not think of it.

"Would you forsake your family and friends to remain with me in Milky Way? You understand my vow never to return to Andromeda. Honor would prohibit me from breaking my oath."

"Does your oath prohibit your loved ones from joining you?"

"I suppose not."

"Then why should it be that they do not come here? For what is a home without family? Your mother and father are distraught from what they believed was your decision to leave Andromeda. They would be delighted to see you and know of your good health. They have searched for you tirelessly; they very nearly commissioned Keid and Arrod to go in search of you, fearing you were deliberately evading them."

"I do not understand. I write to my mother and father often. Surely, they have known my whereabouts at any given time."

"Have you received correspondence in return?"

"No, I have always supposed it was due to the abrupt manner in which I left, believing my family found it unforgivable," Moon reflected with regret.

"Perhaps your letters have been intercepted."

"Helia has always offered to dispatch my letters in company with hers." The notion that she would intentionally neglect to send them confounded Moon exceedingly.

"And what of your most recent letter to me?" Sun inquired. "Did Helia send it for you?"

"No, the letter I composed to you was of too personal a nature to entrust to another, so I dispatched it myself," Moon admitted with candor.

"Helia impeded Keid and Arrod's quest to find you. She wrote that she had seen you, and you were well, traveling with a beautiful companion who she could only assume was your lover."

"She dared to keep me from my family?" Moon inquired, incredulity etched upon his countenance. As he was met with Sun's silence, he continued, "I did not think Helia was capable of such duplicity. She was aware of my parents' effort to locate me and chose to conceal it from me?"

"Yes, Helia is informed. I write to her often to inquire after her adventures."

"Addressing Helia and her deception must wait. What presently occupies my heart is the prospect of solidifying the Vinfinitum Bond with you before any interruptions can occur."

"Come then. We must find Arrod and give him the news."

When Sun and Moon ventured to locate Arrod, a messenger was waiting with a letter.

Dear Sun and Moon,

Do not mistake my disappearance as anything resembling discontent. I am quite delighted about your reunion. As eager as I am to see my old friend, I wish not to disturb you. I can only imagine you have decided to commit yourselves to one another. Undoubtedly, your families shall celebrate the additional ties that will bind your families. Perhaps not all will share in your happiness, though I am sure you are wise of whom I speak.

Miss me not, my friends, I shall return as soon as I settle my affairs in Andromeda. As my two dearest friends find home in Milky Way, so too shall I.

Your faithful friend,

Arrod

Moon felt a pang of disappointment upon discovering Arrod's departure. While he missed his friend, he held onto the hope that Arrod's blessing would infuse their infinity circle with faith.

Lost in thought, Moon was startled when Sun seemed to voice his unspoken thoughts, saying, "I had hoped Arrod would bless our union with faith, but I believe that together, we possess enough of the virtue to complete the ritual."

"We can certainly attempt it, my love," Moon replied, escorting Sun to a secluded place where they could begin the commitment ritual, undisturbed. Despite never hearing of anyone forging the Vinfinitum without external blessings, Moon trusted Sun implicitly. He knew that even if they were to fail, the disappointment would be fleeting, and he would be there to console Sun.

Sun's intuition proved correct as Moon felt the presence of all five virtues swirling around and between them. Within the sanctuary of their infinity circle, they forged the Vinfinitum Bond, founded upon their eternal love, inner strength, enlightening wisdom, unwavering courage, and boundless faith, committing themselves to each other forever.

part six

Unwavering Courage

Helia had vanished soon after Arrod's departure, only to return to Milky Way alongside Draugr and the whole of the five families from Andromeda.

The revelation of Sun and Moon's commitment had Draugr seething with anger, and a low growl emerged from deep within his chest. "You had no right!" he snarled, inching closer to Moon until their personal spaces collided.

Despite Draugr's proximity, Moon maintained his composure, meeting his brother's intense gaze. "Is there something you wish to say, brother?"

"You. Had. No. Right!" Draugr repeated, each word laden with ire. "Sun was promised to me. Our fathers agreed. I gave you a chance to prove Sun returned your affection, but you failed."

"Helia prevented Sun from attending the ceremony that night at your behest," Moon countered, confident that he had acted with honor and integrity. "Do you truly wish to pursue this?"

"That is inconsequential. The agreement had been forged. Sun was to be mine," Draugr hissed, spitting venom as he spoke.

Moon's temper flared at his brother's blatant disregard for Sun. "But she refused you, did she not?" Moon asserted. The tension between him and his brother was palpable, but his resolve was unshakeable. "That's why you sought the agreement before attempting to secure her affection—you knew you'd fail."

"Regardless, the agreement was binding. Unions are arranged all the time. She would have agreed eventually if you had kept your word," Draugr retorted, his face mere inches from Moon's in the tense standoff.

"I kept my word. I never returned to Andromeda. Sun came to me of her own accord," Moon stated firmly, even as Draugr's presence loomed over him.

"After you wrote to her, professing your love for her!"

"I never agreed to abstain from writing, nor did I profess my love for her until long after I departed. The terms of our treaty stipulated that I refrain from declaring my affection for her before or during the celebration, and I adhered to those terms." Moon's eyes locked on his brothers, ready and waiting for him to make a move.

"Gentlemen, enough," their father intervened before violence could ensue. "What's done is done."

"And how shall I be compensated?" Draugr accosted his father, aggressively advancing upon him. "I am to live without my mate, yet no punishment is imposed on the one who stole her from me."

"I will not punish Moon, nor is it any longer within my authority to do so. He is his own man," Moon's father responded.

Draugr then turned to Sun's father, his tone heavy with accusation. "And what of you? Will you punish your daughter for her treasonous act of defiance? I demand retribution."

"Draugr, please. You must understand. You eluded that Sun

returned your affection. I knew not of her affection for Moon," Sun's father argued.

"It matters not! You promised her to me," Draugr forcefully proclaimed, causing his voice to echo through the night like seismic waves.

"Son, what will please you?" Draugr's father asked, concerned as he gazed at his son's determined expression.

"I shall take the power of your virtue and his," Draugr replied, his gaze flickering toward Sun's father with a mix of entitlement and indignation as his features twisted in frustration.

"No!" Sun's cry pierced the aether, her heart pounding with dread at the thought of such an unreasonable demand. Any compensation would be unfathomable, considering the deceit employed to garner the commitment agreement from the start.

"You could dissolve your union with my brother and create the Vinfinitum Bond with me," Draugr proposed to Sun with longing and urgency. The tremble in his voice betrayed a hint of desperation.

Sun's eyes narrowed with fierce tenacity. "I would never!" Her response was swift and unyielding.

"Then this is my demand," Draugr insisted through clenched teeth, rage flashing through his countenance as he confronted Sun and her father.

"Draugr, please be reasonable." Strained with emotion, Draugr's father interjected, pleading with him to see their perspective.

"Two powers, one each from the fathers of two willful spirits, seems fair to me," he replied, his countenance shifting unnervingly to an icy resolve, sending a chill down their spines as they realized the depth of his determination.

After much deliberation, the fathers ultimately agreed to Draugr's terms, much to Sun and Moon's dismay. Thus, Draugr was bestowed with the Divine Gifts associated with the virtues of wisdom, strength, and courage. He had become the most power-ful celestial being in all the universe, apart only from the Divine themselves.

Draugr and Helia left Milky Way, as neither could endure the constant reminder of their siblings' love.

After several years, Moon called for a joyous gathering. "Dearest family and friends, Sun and I have gathered you all here today to share some wonderful news," he said as he gazed at Sun fondly. "We are overjoyed to introduce our daughter to you. From the depths of our love, a new planet has been born; we have named her Earth."

Amidst the warm wishes of health and happiness from their loved ones, Moon beseeched them to withhold their congratulations. "Thank you, but there is more to our announcement," he continued. "Earth is a unique and remarkable planet, imbued with an abundance of strength and wisdom. She possesses the powers of both virtues."

Their audience was captivated by the revelation, but Moon pressed on. "And there's more... new forms of life have emerged on her surface."

A wave of disbelief swept through the guests. "It's true. Earth is teeming with diverse life," Sun interjected. "Among them, the largest, most dominant, and most multifarious, we call "Dinosaurs.""

The news of Earth's birth and the vibrant life upon her surface spread swiftly across the universe, eventually reaching Draugr and Helia. Draugr returned to Milky Way, issuing an ultimatum to Sun. He demanded that she sever her bond with Moon and take what he claimed was her rightful place by his side, threatening to destroy Earth along with her inhabitants if she refused.

Sun rejected Draugr's ultimatum immediately. However, loyal in their love and devotion to their daughter, Sun and Moon made a solemn decision. Though they would not sacrifice their Vinfinitum Bond, they pledged to protect Earth at any cost. Thus, Sun vowed to protect Earth by day, while Moon swore to watch over her by night.

Millions of Earthly years passed, with Sun and Moon exchanging fleeting glances at dusk and dawn. Despite their profound longing for each other, they found solace in their shared commitment to protect their cherished daughter while loving each other from afar.

As Draugr's fury intensified, he eventually acted on his ominous threat to destroy Sun and Moon's daughter. Utilizing his immense power, he propelled a colossal asteroid toward Earth. The impact was catastrophic, inflicting grave harm and thrusting numerous lifeforms into extinction.

Realizing that mere vigilance from afar was inadequate, Sun felt compelled to go to Earth. Convinced that Draugr would hesitate to harm her daughter if it meant endangering her in the process, she devised a perilous plan to relinquish her celestial star form and assume a physical incarnation suitable for surviving on Earth's surface.

With steadfast determination, she was resolved to thwart Draugr's malevolent intentions.

Moon adamantly refused to entertain the notion of Sun embarking on such a precarious journey alone, insisting that they must face the danger together. Sun argued, stressing the importance of Moon remaining behind to safeguard Earth in case her endeavor failed.

In response, Moon asserted that he would go, so Sun could

remain safe with their family in Milky Way. However, Sun countered by proclaiming that Draugr would be even more motivated to harm Earth if he inhabited her surface alone.

Having sacrificed all he could, Moon emphasized his need to be by her side. He implored her to allow them to confront the risk together and entrust their beloved Earth's protection to their clan if they did not survive.

Sun shared Moon's reluctance to be separated. However, she could not fathom a way for them to remain together. She understood that time would pass differently on Earth. Even a momentary delay in their descent could equate to years passing on Earth due to the planet's unique time dilation.

Adopting physical forms suitable for Earth's surface without depleting her resources would make it impossible for them to locate each other amidst Earth's vastness. The necessary forms would be small and inconspicuous.

Moon fully comprehended Sun's fears, but he also had boundless faith in their love and the efficacy of her Divine gift, which enabled her to cultivate love when combined with the love in her heart. Believing their love could empower her to achieve unprecedented feats, Moon persuaded Sun to embark on the endeavor of forging a new bond that would coalesce their spirits, bonding them on Earth and in the cosmos.

He was sure she could create a new bond that would render them inseparable or, at the very least, provide them with some means of locating each other from anywhere on Earth.

Upon searching her heart, Sun knew Moon was right. She could conjure such a bond.

Unlike the Bond of Faith, Vinfinitum, her bond would be a Bond of Love. The process would be arduous, requiring them to gradually complete the entirety of the bond in stages.

First, they would coalesce their hearts with a bond she named Vinis. Next, they would unite their bodies with the Vincuis, followed by their minds with the Vintate, their souls with the Vina, and finally, their spirits with the Viidivus, holistically completing the Bonds of Love.

In contrast to the Bond of Faith, once all five Bonds of Love were forged, culminating with the Viidivus, they would not only be eternal but also utterly unbreakable, coalescing their hearts, bodies, minds, souls, and spirits for all eternity with no possibility of reversal.

Moon adamantly asserted that he would only consent to the risky venture if they confronted it together. Thus, prompted by her endless love for Moon, Sun poured her heart into crafting the Bonds of Love. Their deep affection for each other and the blessings of all five sacred virtues within them empowered the process.

After completing the heartfelt endeavor that irrevocably coalesced the entirety of their beings to one another for all eternity, Sun and Moon relinquished their celestial forms. Embracing mortal incarnations tailored for life on Earth, they descended with unwavering courage to their daughter's surface, arriving poised to fulfill their roles as her guardians.

The End

acknowledgements

For my beloved mother,

In the pages of my life, you are the most beautiful chapter, written with love, strength, wisdom, and unwavering faith. This is a humble tribute to the profound imprint you've left on my soul. If not for you, I wouldn't dare have the courage to dream.

For my loving husband,

Your presence ignites a fire within me. Your belief in me has pushed me beyond my comfort zone, guiding me through challenges and triumphs alike. I am endlessly grateful for your unwavering support, propelling me to chase after my passions with determination.

For my cherished daughter,

Your wisdom transcends your years. You've taught me that dreaming is not only permissible but an obligation to my heart. Your steadfast expectation that I nurture myself has guided my pursuit of those dreams. I owe you endless gratitude for instilling in me the strength to reach for the stars.

For my treasured son,

My eternal dreamer, your boundless love and curiosity in my dreams reflect the encouragement and motivation you've bestowed upon me. As my faithful partner in the journey through my world, you are truly my beacon of inspiration. I'll forever treasure the motivation you've ignited within my soul.

For my precious niece,

Your wholehearted embrace of my vulnerable dreams has empowered me to refine and nurture them. Your unwavering support has granted me the bravery to embrace my truest self, guiding me through uncertain times. Without you, I might never have found the strength to press onward.

For my dear sister,

Amidst life's bustling chaos, your subtle gestures and kindness have truly defined our bond. Your small acts of faith have silently paved the path for my dreams, inspiring me to aim for the moon. You are my unsung hero, and I am endlessly grateful for the profound impact you've had on my journey.

ABOUT THE AUTHOR

Katie Monohan

is a fantasy romance author from the Pacific Northwest, with a heart rooted in origin stories and a soul that dances between worlds—both magical and real. A proud Native American, she draws deep inspiration from her cultural heritage, especially the storytelling traditions passed down through generations. This love of legends and beginnings sparked The Legend of Sun and Moon, the enchanting prelude to her Celestial Bonds of Love series.

By day, Katie is an accountant—a lover of logic, spreadsheets, and structure. By night, she transforms into a weaver of worlds, where sacred virtues take form, celestial bonds shape destinies, and eternal love lights every page. For her, writing is more than storytelling—it's sanctuary. A way to give voice to the emotions she's lived and craft stories that connect with readers on both emotional and imaginative levels.

When she's not writing or wrangling numbers, Katie spends her time with her incredibly supportive husband, her two amazing teenagers—a daughter in college and a son in high school—and her fur-babies: Luna, a fiercely loyal white German Shepherd, and Gypsy, a black-and-white cat with enough charm (and attitude) to inspire a novel of his own.

Thank you

for spending time in this world with me. *The Legend of Sun and Moon* was written as a sacred beginning—a myth whispered between stars, rooted in the kind of love that transcends time, pain, and separation.

If this story stirred something in you—if it made you feel seen, softened, or sovereign—I'd be honored if you shared that feeling with others. A short review helps indie authors like me reach the readers who need these stories most.

And if you're ready for more... the legacy of this love lives on in *Sun's Heart: Love for Two Knights*, coming soon.

With love and moonlight,

Katie Monohan

More stories await...

Be the first to receive exclusive reveals, bonus scenes, and news about special events by joining my newsletter.

Newsletter: Subscribe here:

katiemonohan.com/subscribe-hc

You can also find me at:

Website: Step into my romantasy realm

katiemonohan.com

Instagram: Follow

instagram.com/katie.monohan

Facebook: Join the community

facebook.com/LegendSunMoon

Tik Tok: Watch behind the scenes

tiktok.com/@katie.monohan

And that was just the beginning...

Legends never really end. Do they?

They thread themselves through blood and breath—through time and touch—until one day, they choose someone new to remember them.

For a sneak peek into

Sun's Heart

turn the page.

Love for Two Knights

PROLOGUE

Azalea

The carnival smelled of sugar and blood the day an angel pulled me from the clutches of darkness. Laughter rang out over the carousel, bright and childlike, even as screams ripped out of my chest.

What I am—what I've always been—is something both coveted and cursed. Before I could even grasp the danger that hunted me, Noctareans found me.

I was five years old when the life I knew unraveled, and another emerged. I crossed the *veil* between innocence and knowledge, no longer shielded by the fragile illusions of childhood. Evil creatures lurked in the shadows. The boogeyman was real, serving demons older than nightmares.

But angels were no myth, either—or at least that's what I thought when I first saw Atreyus.

But he wasn't an angel. He was a Guardian—a celestial being who sacrificed his cosmic form to protect Earth and her inhabitants from destruction.

What began as a day of laughter, cotton candy, and carnival rides became a nightmare etched in blood. By the end, my parents lay dead, and my white dress was crimson, hot, and slick with my angel's sacrifice.

Noctareans weren't after my family—my parents were merely casualties in their relentless pursuit of me.

And my angel—he didn't have to save me. But he stepped out from the shadows, his downy-white, silver-tipped wings radiant against the darkness. With the grace of a celestial warrior and a valor far beyond his years, he gave everything to keep me alive.

But then everything I held dear vanished:

My parents.

My world.

My angel.

KATIE MONOHAN
ROMANTASY AUTHOR
CRAFTING DREAMS WHERE MAGIC & PASSION UNITE